THE DINOSAUR THAT POOPED THE PAST!

Check out Danny and Dinosaur in more adventures:

THE DINOSAUR THAT POOPED CHRISTMAS
THE DINOSAUR THAT POOPED A PLANET!
THE DINOSAUR THAT POOPED THE BED!

To the asteroid that wiped out the dinosaurs . . . not cool dude, not cool . . . – T.F. & D.P.

For baby Kyle – G.P.

RED FOX

UK | USA | Canada | Ireland | Australia
India | New Zealand | South Africa

Red Fox is part of the Penguin Random House group of companies
whose addresses can be found at global.penguinrandomhouse.com.

www.penguin.co.uk   www.puffin.co.uk   www.ladybird.co.uk

Penguin
Random House
UK

First published by Red Fox 2014
Book and CD edition published 2015, reissued 2017
002

Copyright © Tom Fletcher and Dougie Poynter, 2014
Illustrated by Garry Parsons
The moral right of the authors and illustrator has been asserted

Audio recording produced by Samantha Halstead
Editing and special effects by Richard Hughes

Printed in China

A CIP catalogue record for this book is available from the British Library

ISBN: 978–1–782–95484–2

FSC
www.fsc.org
MIX
Paper from
responsible sources
FSC® C018179

THE DINOSAUR THAT POOPED THE PAST!

Tom Fletcher and Dougie Poynter
Illustrated by Garry Parsons

RED FOX

Some grannies are old, some grannies are great,
And Danny's was turning one thousand and eight.
He sang "HAPPY BIRTHDAY" with Dinosaur too,
Then asked to go out: there was playing to do!

"You cannot go out till your plates are all clean!"
Said Granny while serving up sludge that was green.
There were broccoli eggs and hard Brussels sprouts —
The dinosaur slopped the lot into its mouth.

Then in the two seconds when Gran wasn't looking,
It ate Danny's pile of awful Gran-cooking.

"Well done!" Granny said. "You've eaten enough.
Now you can go out and do awesome cool stuff!"

They ran straight to the tree with a swing underneath,
But it hadn't been swung since Gran lost her teeth.
They swung back and forth, they went up, they went down.
"Higher!" Dan said. "Let's go all the way round!"

But this wasn't an ordinary swing; it had powers –
     Powers to turn back the minutes and hours!
They counted to three and pushed hard off the ground.
     They looped and they looped and they turned time around.

Their heads went all dizzy, time started to bend,
So Danny held on to his dinosaur friend!
Flashes and fizzes and sparkly squeaks,
They swung past the Romans, Egyptians and Greeks.

Then, with a **CRACK,** the swing snapped in half . . .

. . . They crash-landed into a land from the past,
Surrounded by trees of Jurassical size,
Being watched through the leaves by mischievous eyes.

Then three baby dinos jumped down awesomely,
Who called themselves Dino Dudes A, B and C,
They liked playing games like stackety-stack,
Where Dino Dudes A and B climb on C's back!

Then suddenly Dinosaur's
tummy made grumbles –
Grumbles and rumbles that
made the ground crumble.
But grounds do not crumble
for any old reason,
Grounds only crumble in
VOLCANO SEASON!

"We swung back in time, we were trying to play,"
Said Danny to Dino Dudes B, C and A.
"We need to get back, we need to leave fast,
We need to get everyone out of the past!"

But Danny and Dinosaur's only way back
   Was looping through time on the swing that had snapped!

The lava was coming, the lava was hot –
   Even hotter than Granny's old veg-cooking pot!

And so, without thinking, B, C and A
    Stacked themselves up like the game that they play –
But this wasn't a game, it was saving the day.
    Saving the day the Dino-Dude way!

They flipped and they jumped through the jungle with ease,
Surfing the lava on lava-proof leaves,
Gathering all of the things they would need
To fix the time-swing at the speediest speed!

Wax from the bees, sap from the trees,
A tusk that fell off when an old mammoth sneezed,
They bashed it together with stegosaur teeth,
While dodging explosive eruptions beneath.

The swing had been fixed, but the dinosaur group
Were now far too heavy to time-travel loop.
Dan started to worry, then started to panic —
The ground underneath was now hot and volcanic!

They all started crying, they cried and they cried,
They cried, and their tears instantly vaporised.

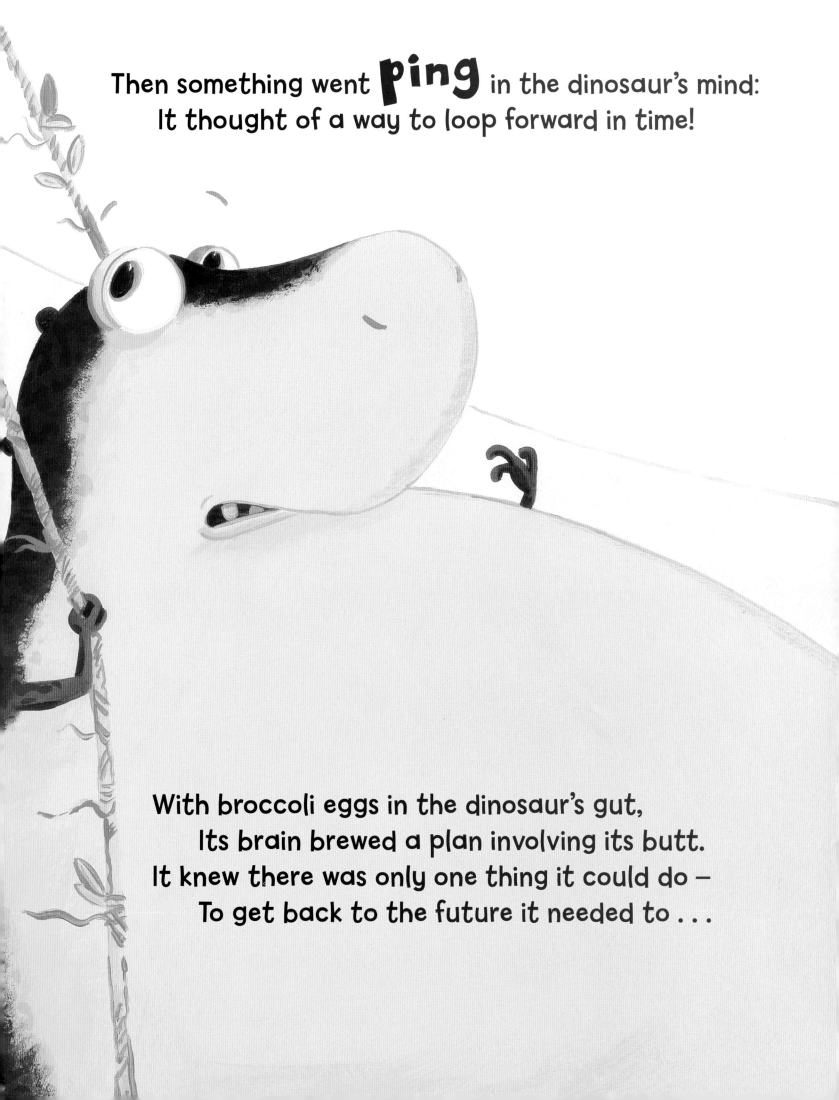

Then something went **ping** in the dinosaur's mind:
It thought of a way to loop forward in time!

With broccoli eggs in the dinosaur's gut,
Its brain brewed a plan involving its butt.
It knew there was only one thing it could do —
To get back to the future it needed to . . .

POO!

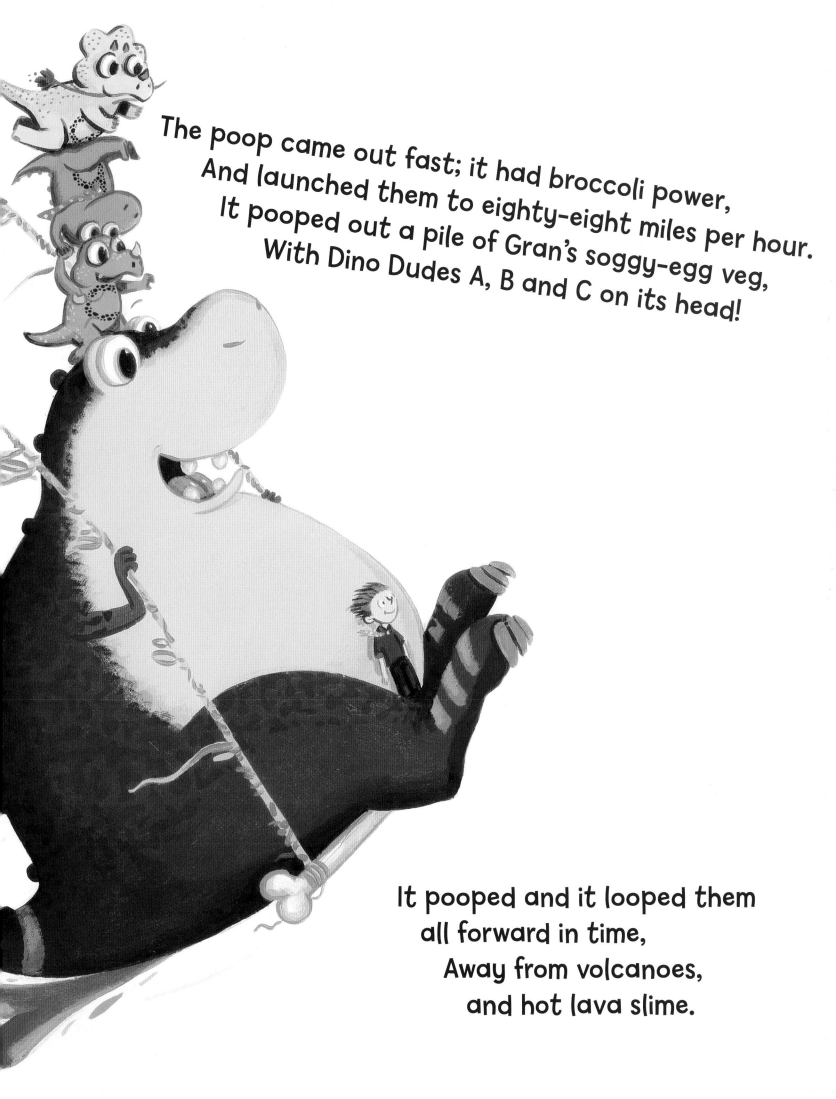

The poop came out fast; it had broccoli power,
And launched them to eighty-eight miles per hour.
It pooped out a pile of Gran's soggy-egg veg,
With Dino Dudes A, B and C on its head!

It pooped and it looped them
all forward in time,
Away from volcanoes,
and hot lava slime.

The Romans and Trojans were covered in poop;
They all got a taste of Gran's broccoli soup.

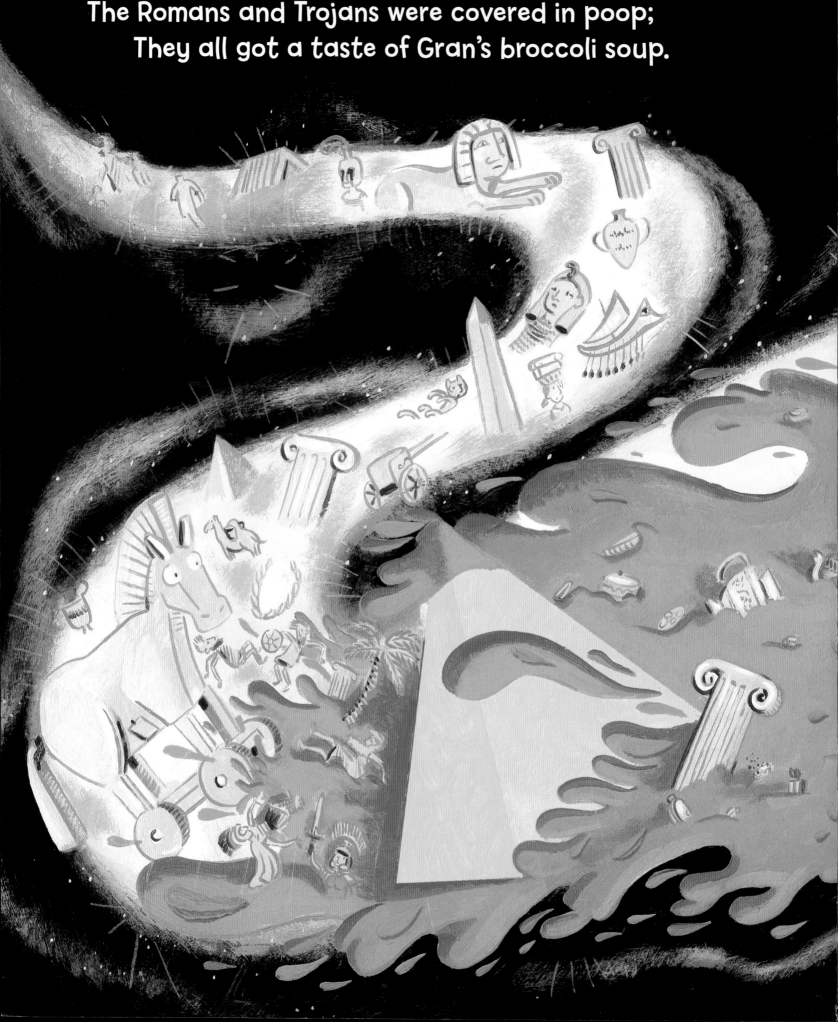

Whilst looping through Egypt, it pooped out a pile
Which made a poop pyramid next to the Nile.
It plopped out the sprouts, its bum did a smelly,
And looped out the last piece of poop from its belly.

They fell out of time, they'd made it back home,
But Danny and Dinosaur weren't on their own . . .
Dino Dudes A, B and C were there too –
They'd travelled through time on the broccoli poo!

They all started cheering and jumping around,
    It seemed like new dinosaur friends had been found!

. . . and just when they'd had all the veg they could take,
Birthday Gran served up her broccoli cake!